Here's what kids have to say to
Mary Pope Osborne, author of
the Magic Tree House series:

*I think Jack and Annie are the best book
characters in the world.*—Thomas V.

*I love your books so much, I feel like putting an
"M" on the floor of my tree house.*—Nathan W.

*I really love your books. Once I start them, I
can never put them down till I'm done.*—Pam W.

*I love your books so much, I want to keep them
locked in a safe where no one can get to them
but me.*—Danny A.

I like your books a lot, and I mean a lot.
—Johanna S.

*I love your books. I think about them so much
that when I go to sleep I dream I'm in the
story. It's really exciting, and it's never a
nightmare.*—Joan P.

*I wish I could spend my life reading the Magic
Tree House series.*—Juliette S.

*I'm only allowed to check out two books, and I
always check out two Magic Tree House
books.*—Max B.

Librarians and teachers love
Magic Tree House books, too!

My class is spinning with excitement over the Magic Tree House series. I can't get the books fast enough.—K. Mahanes

We use the Magic Tree House books for whole group reading, silent reading, and cooperative learning. [My students] have been "taken around the world" through this series.—M. Woodson

The Magic Tree House stories have been a motivating factor in developing lifelong readers and writers.—B. Rosen

Our school library has a hard time keeping any of the books on the shelf. The only problem I see with this series is that there are not enough books in it. Keep writing, Ms. Osborne!—J. Landsteiner

We have the best time reading the Magic Tree House series. Jack and Annie have become household names.—K. Moore

You should have been in the classroom when I discovered and shared with them that there were indeed four more [books]. They literally stood and cheered.—C. Garrison

[My students] choose your books to reread during free time, which is the greatest compliment of all.—N. Ruud

Your books have become so popular in our school that the shelf life of one of your books is about five seconds.—C. Dailey

Dear Readers,

Hour of the Olympics was a joy for me to write, mostly because Jack and Annie meet my favorite creature of Greek mythology.

I've been very interested in the Greek myths for many years. In fact, I've written a number of different books retelling them, including several picture books.

My hope is that Hour of the Olympics will help spark _your_ interest in Greek mythology. Though these stories were first told over three thousand years ago, they are still some of the most vibrant, exciting tales we have today. When we read them, it's as if we're listening to the ancient Greek storytellers across the centuries. Now that's _real_ time travel, don't you think?

All my best,

Mary Pope Osborne

Hour of the Olympics

by Mary Pope Osborne
illustrated by Sal Murdocca

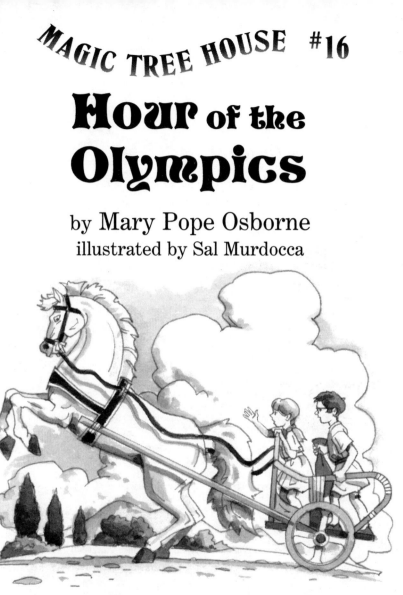

A STEPPING STONE BOOK™

Random House 🏠 New York

To Chase Goddard,
who loves to read

Random House gives special thanks to Jonathan Master for providing
the Greek spelling of "Pegasus."

www.randomhouse.com/kids

Library of Congress Cataloging-in-Publication Data

Osborne, Mary Pope.
Hour of the Olympics / by Mary Pope Osborne ; illustrated by Sal Murdocca.
p. cm. — (Magic tree house ; #16) "A Stepping Stone book." Summary: Their
magic tree house takes Jack and Annie back to retrieve a lost story in ancient
Greece, where they witness the original Olympic games and are surprised to find
what girls of the time were not allowed to do.

ISBN 0-679-89062-9 (pbk.) — ISBN 0-679-99062-3 (lib. bdg.)
[1. Olympics—Fiction. 2. Greece—Fiction. 3. Time travel—Fiction. 4. Sex role—
Fiction. 5. Magic—Fiction. 6. Tree houses—Fiction.]
I. Murdocca, Sal, ill. II. Title. III. Series: Osborne, Mary Pope. Magic tree house
series ; 16. PZ7.081167Ho 1998 [Fic]—dc21 98-24100

Printed in the United States of America 10 9 8 7 6 5 4 3 2

Random House, Inc. New York, Toronto, London, Sydney, Auckland

A STEPPING STONE BOOK is a trademark of Random House, Inc.

Contents

Prologue

One summer day in Frog Creek, Pennsylvania, a mysterious tree house appeared in the woods.

Eight-year-old Jack and his seven-year-old sister, Annie, climbed into the tree house. They found that it was filled with books.

Jack and Annie soon discovered that the tree house was magic. It could take them to the places in the books. All they had to do was to point to a picture and wish to go there.

Along the way, they discovered that the tree house belongs to Morgan le Fay. Morgan is a magical librarian from the time of King Arthur. She travels through time and space, gathering books.

In the Magic Tree House Books #8–12, Jack and Annie solved four ancient riddles and became Master Librarians. To help them in their future tasks, Morgan gave Jack and Annie secret library cards with the letters **M L** on them.

Jack and Annie's first four missions are to save stories from ancient libraries. This is their fourth mission...

1

Just One More

"You awake?" Annie's voice came out of the dark.

"Yep," said Jack from his bed.

"Get up," said Annie. "We have to get to the tree house before sunrise."

"I'm ready," said Jack.

He threw back his covers and jumped out of bed. He was wearing his jeans and T-shirt.

"You slept in your clothes?" asked Annie.

"I didn't want to waste any time," said

Jack. He pulled on his backpack.

Annie laughed.

"You must really be excited about going to ancient Greece," she said.

"Yep," said Jack.

"Do you have your secret library card?" asked Annie.

"Yeah, do you?" said Jack.

"Sure. Put it in your backpack," she said. She handed her card to him. "I'll carry the flashlight."

"All set," said Jack.

They tiptoed downstairs and out the door.

Outside the air was fresh and cool.

"There's no moon," said Annie. "Just stars."

She turned on her flashlight.

"Ta-da!" she said. "Let's go."

They followed the beam of light across their yard and up the street.

Jack was thrilled to be going to ancient Greece. But something worried him.

"What do you think will happen after we go to Greece?" he asked Annie. "Is this our last mission ever?"

"Oh, I hope not," said Annie. "What do you think?"

"I don't know. Let's ask Morgan," said Jack.

"Hurry!" said Annie.

They started running. The flashlight beam flew in front of them, lighting the way.

They slowed to a walk when they got to the Frog Creek woods. The thick woods were pitch-black.

Annie shined the flashlight upward as

they walked between the trees. Finally, they found the magic tree house.

"We're here!" Annie called.

"Go on up," said Jack.

Annie grabbed the rope ladder and started up. Jack followed.

Annie shined the flashlight around the tree house.

Morgan le Fay was sitting at the window. She covered her eyes when the light hit her face.

"Turn off the light, please, Annie," she said softly.

Annie turned it off.

"Welcome," Morgan said in the dark. "Are you ready for your next mission?"

"Yes!" said Annie. Then her voice got quiet. "This isn't our last one ever, is it?"

"Ask me that question *after* this mission," said Morgan.

"We want to go on more," said Jack.

"You're very brave to say that," said Morgan. "You've had three very hard journeys as Master Librarians."

"Oh, they weren't so hard," said Jack.

"You risked your life to save the lost story of Hercules," said Morgan.

"It was nothing," said Annie.

"*And* the Chinese story of the silk weaver," said Morgan. "And the Irish story of the serpent monster Sarph. Thank you."

"You're welcome," said Jack and Annie.

"Now," said Morgan, "for the last story..."

Jack heard a rustling sound.

"Here is the title," Morgan said. "You can shine your light on it, Annie."

Annie turned the flashlight back on. She shined it on the paper.

ΠΙΓΑΣΟΣ

"Wow, is that Greek?" asked Jack.

"It certainly is," said Morgan.

She reached into her robe again and pulled out a book.

"For your research," she said.

Jack took the book from her. Annie shined her flashlight on the cover. They read the title: *A Day in Ancient Greece*.

"Now, what must you always remember?" asked Morgan.

"Our research book will guide us," said Jack.

"But in our darkest hour, only the lost story can save us," said Annie.

Morgan nodded. "And you must show your secret library cards to the wisest person you meet," she said.

"Don't worry. We will. Bye!" said Annie.

Jack shivered with excitement as he pointed at the book's cover.

"I wish we could go there," he said.

"And I wish we could go on lots of other missions!" Annie added.

The wind began to blow.

The tree house started to spin.

It spun faster and faster.

Then everything was silent.

Absolutely silent.

2

Any Girls Here?

Jack opened his eyes. Warm sunshine streamed into the tree house.

"We sure don't need the flashlight here," he said.

"Look, Morgan gave us clothes like the ones we wore in Pompeii," said Annie.

Jack looked down.

His clothes *were* similar to the ones he'd worn in the Roman town of Pompeii: a tunic and sandals. He also had a leather bag in place of his backpack again.

Annie looked out the window.

"And we landed in an olive tree—just like Pompeii!" said Annie.

Jack looked out the window. He caught his breath.

"Are we in the wrong place?" he asked.

"I don't know," said Annie. "Look past the trees. Doesn't it look like a big fair?"

Jack looked. Annie was right. Past the olive grove was a field filled with white tents. Beyond the field were red-brick buildings with columns and huge crowds of people.

"What's going on?" Jack asked.

He pulled the research book out of his leather bag. He found a picture of the scene outside. Below the picture were these words:

**The Olympic Games began in ancient
Greece over 2,500 years ago. Every
four years, more than 40,000 people
traveled to Olympia, the town where
the festival of athletic games took
place.**

"Oh, man," Jack whispered. "We're at the
ancient Olympics!"

"Cool," said Annie.

Jack wrote in his notebook:

*Olympia—
first Olympics take place*

"Come on, let's go watch!" Annie said. She
started down the rope ladder.

Jack threw his notebook and the research
book into his leather bag.

"Don't forget we have to get Morgan's

story, too," he said as he followed Annie.

Annie waited as Jack stepped to the ground. Then they walked through the olive grove to where the tents were.

Jack heard pipe music and smelled food roasting over fires. Groups of men talked excitedly to one another.

"That's funny," said Annie. "I don't see any girls here."

"Oh, sure, there're girls," said Jack.

"Where?" said Annie. "Show me."

Jack looked around. But he only saw men and boys—no women or girls at all.

Then he saw an outdoor theater. A woman was standing on the stage. She had yellow hair and a purple tunic.

"There," said Jack, pointing.

"What's she doing?" asked Annie.

A soldier was on the stage with her. He wore a long cape. A helmet with a red crest hid his face.

The woman and the soldier were waving their arms and talking loudly to each other.

"I think they're doing a play," said Jack. "I'll look."

He pulled out the Greek book and found a picture of the theater.

"Listen," he said. He read aloud:

**The Greeks were the first to write
plays. Many English words for the
theater come from Greek words, such
as *drama, scenery,* and *chorus.* Many
Greek plays are still performed today.**

"Hey, Jack," said Annie. "You're wrong."

When Jack looked up, he saw the woman
had pulled off her wig. It was a boy dressed
up as a woman!

"See, even *she's* a boy," said Annie. "That's
weird."

"Hmm," said Jack. He went on reading:

**A few actors would play many differ-
ent parts in the same play. Women
were not allowed to act, so men played
the female roles, too.**

"That's not fair," said Annie. "What if a

woman *wanted* to be in a play?"

"Don't worry about it," said Jack. He put the book away. "Let's just take a peek at the Olympics, then find our story."

He nudged Annie to move along.

Just then he heard a voice.

"Wait!"

They turned around. A man with a short white beard was walking toward them.

"Hello," said the man. He was looking right at Annie. "Who are you?"

"Who are *you?*" Annie asked boldly.

17

3

The Secret Poet

The bearded man smiled at Annie.

"My name is Plato," he said.

"Plato?" said Jack. That name sounded familiar.

"You may have heard of me," the man said. "I am a philosopher."

"What's that mean?" said Annie.

"A lover of wisdom," said Plato.

"Wow," said Annie.

Plato smiled at her.

"It's odd to see a girl walking so bravely through Olympia," he said. "You must be from far away."

"We're Jack and Annie," said Annie. "And we come from Frog Creek, Pennsylvania. It's *very* far away."

Plato looked puzzled.

Annie turned to Jack.

"I think we should show him our cards," she said in a low voice. "He's a lover of wisdom."

Jack nodded. He reached into his bag and took out the secret library cards. He showed them to Plato.

The letters **M** and **L** that stood for Master Librarian glittered on the cards.

"Amazing!" said Plato. "I've never met such young Master Librarians. Why have you come to Olympia?"

Jack pulled out the piece of paper with the title of the story.

"We're looking for this story," he said.

ΠΊΓΑΣΟΣ

"Oh, yes," said Plato softly. "This was written by a brilliant poet—a friend of mine, in fact."

"Do you know where the poet lives?" asked Jack.

"Very near here," said Plato.

"Will you take us there?" asked Annie.

"Yes, but I must warn you—never tell anyone who the poet is," said Plato. "It's a secret."

"We won't," whispered Annie.

Plato led them away from the outdoor theater.

They started down a dirt road. It was crowded with people heading to the games.

Plato stopped at the door of a sand-colored house with a brick roof.

He opened the door and led Jack and Annie into an empty courtyard.

"Wait here," he said. He disappeared through a doorway.

Jack and Annie looked around.

Rooms opened onto the sunny courtyard. Everything was quiet.

"The people who live here must have gone to the games," said Annie.

"I bet you're right," said Jack.

He pulled out the Greek book and found a picture of a house. He read aloud:

Men and women lived in separate parts of a Greek house. Women spent

most of their time spinning and
weaving and taking care of the kitchen.
Boys were sent away to school when
they were seven. Girls were not
allowed to go to school.

"Girls can't go to school?" said Annie. "How do they learn to read and write?"

At that moment Plato returned. With him was a young woman dressed in a long tunic with a colored border. She was holding a scroll.

Annie smiled a big smile.

"*Finally,*" she said. "Another girl."

"Jack and Annie, meet our secret poet," said Plato.

4

Not Fair!

The young woman smiled at Jack and Annie.

"How did you learn to read and write?" Annie asked.

"I taught myself," the woman answered.

"She wrote a poem and brought it to me," said Plato, "because I have written and told people that I think Greek girls *should* go to school and learn things."

"Is that the poem?" said Jack. He pointed to the poet's scroll.

"Yes," said the young woman.

"It's a wonderful story," said Plato. "But she will get in trouble if it is read in our land. You must take it back to your faraway home, where it will be safe."

The poet handed Jack her scroll. He put it into his backpack.

"Tell us your name," said Annie. "So we can tell people who wrote the story."

The young woman shook her head.

"I cannot," she said. When she saw Annie's sad face, she added, "You can tell people it was written by Anonymous."

"*That's* your name?" asked Annie.

"No, *anonymous* means that no one knows who wrote it," said Plato.

"But that's not true!" said Annie.

"I'm afraid the risk is too great," said Plato.

Annie looked back at the woman.

"I'm sorry," said Annie. "It's not fair—not at all."

The poet smiled at her. "I am happy that

you will take my story to your country," she said. "Perhaps someday women everywhere will write books just like men."

"They will," said Jack. "I promise."

The young woman looked at him, puzzled.

"It's true!" said Annie.

"Thank you, Annie," the young woman said. "And thank you, Jack." She bowed, then hurried out of the courtyard.

"Wait!" said Annie.

She started to go after the poet, but Plato stopped her.

"Come along," he said. "The games will start soon."

Plato then led Jack and Annie out of the Greek house back onto the dirt road.

"Girls can't write stories," grumbled Annie. "They can't go to school. They can't be in plays. I've had enough of ancient Greece. Let's get out of here."

"Wait," said Jack. "What about the Olympics?"

"Oh, yeah," said Annie. Her eyes got brighter. "I almost forgot."

"Well," said Plato slowly. "I would like to take you both to the games. I have special seats in the viewing box. However..." He looked at Annie.

"Don't tell me," she said. "Girls can't go to the Olympics either."

Plato shook his head.

"A girl will get in terrible trouble if she goes to the games," he said.

Annie sighed. "It's really, *really* not fair," she said.

"I'm sorry," said Plato. "My country is a

democracy. We believe in freedom for our citizens. But I'm afraid right now that only means men."

"Annie's right. It's not fair," said Jack. "I think we should go home now."

"No, Jack. *You* go to the Olympics," said Annie. "At least you can tell me about it. Take notes."

"What about you?" Jack said.

"I'll go back to that play at the outdoor theater," Annie said. "Meet me there when you're done."

Jack didn't want to leave Annie alone. But he also didn't want to miss the Olympics.

"Go! Have fun!" Annie said. She began walking away. "I'll see you later! Bye, Plato!"

"Bye, Annie," said Plato.

Annie turned back again and waved.

"I'll tell you all about it!" Jack called.

"This way," said Plato.

He and Jack turned and joined the crowd heading toward the Olympic grounds.

5

Hi, Zeus

"This is the very first day of the games," Plato told Jack, "the day of the chariot races."

"Oh, wow," whispered Jack.

He couldn't believe he was going to see a chariot race. The modern Olympic Games didn't have chariot races.

They walked toward the race track. Plato pointed to a large building near the road.

"That is the gymnasium," he said. "It is where our athletes train. They practice running and throwing the javelin and discus."

"We have a gymnasium at our school in Frog Creek," said Jack. "We call it a gym."

"People all over the world copy us Greeks," Plato said.

"Wait," said Jack. "I have to take notes for Annie."

He pulled out his notebook and wrote:

Ancient Greeks invented gyms

"Okay, we can go," said Jack. He tucked his notebook under his arm.

As they moved along, Plato pointed to a beautiful tree nearby.

"The olive tree is our sacred tree," he said. "The winners of the games will wear crowns made from its branches."

"Oh, wow," said Jack. And he wrote:

Olive tree is sacred

Next they passed a beautiful statue of a winged lady.

"Who's that?" said Jack.

"She's Nike, the goddess of victory," said Plato.

Jack quickly wrote:

Nike is goddess of victory

"Nike is important to the games," said Plato. "But the most important Olympic god is in there."

He took Jack to a brick building with huge columns. They stepped through the door. It was a temple. Jack gasped.

In front of them loomed the biggest statue he had ever seen.

The statue was at least two stories high. It was a bearded man sitting on a throne.

"This is the temple of Zeus. And that is a statue of Zeus himself," said Plato. "The Olympic Games are played in his honor. He is the chief god of the Greek gods and goddesses."

"Oh, man," whispered Jack.

"Yesterday all the athletes came here," said Plato. "They swore to Zeus that they had trained for ten months. And they promised to obey the rules of the games."

The statue of the mighty Greek god stared down at Jack.

Jack felt very small.

"Hi, Zeus," he said. His voice was small, too.

Suddenly, trumpet sounds came from outside.

"The hour has come," said Plato. "We must hurry. The Olympic parade begins!"

6

Mystery Man

Plato and Jack hurried past the crowds standing at the sides of the race track. Everyone was shouting and cheering.

"I have seats next to the judges," said Plato. He pointed to a tall stand with rows of benches.

Plato led Jack through the crowd and up the steps to their seats.

"Wow, thanks," said Jack.

He had a great view.

The Olympic parade had already started. Musicians playing pipes were at the front. Behind them marched the Olympic athletes —the best in all of Greece.

Jack sighed as he watched the parade going around the track. *Annie would really love this*, he thought.

"The athletes in front are the runners," said Plato. "Foot races are the oldest event of the Olympics."

Jack pulled out his notebook and wrote:

oldest event is foot races

"Behind the runners are the boxers," said Plato. "They're wearing special gloves and bronze helmets."

Jack wrote:

boxers wear gloves and helmets

"Behind them are the wrestlers," said Plato.

And Jack wrote:

wrestlers

When Jack looked up again, he saw a soldier staring up at him from the sidelines.

The soldier was dressed like the actor from the outdoor theater. He had on a long cape and a red-crested helmet that covered most of his face.

But something was strange. This soldier was short—*really* short.

"Here come the discus and javelin throwers," said Plato, "and then the men in armor."

"What do they do?" asked Jack.

"They race wearing full armor," said Plato.

Jack smiled to himself. He knew Annie would think that was funny.

He wrote in his notebook:

Some runners race in armor

Jack finished writing.

He looked back at the short soldier.

"In a moment, the chariot races will begin," said Plato. "Winning a chariot race is the greatest honor of the games."

Jack just nodded. He was still studying the short soldier, who seemed to be looking back at him.

Suddenly, a small hand came out from the soldier's cape. The hand gave a little wave.

Jack gasped. It was Annie's hand waving!

The short soldier was *Annie*.

7

Go! Go! Go!

Jack stared in horror at Annie. She must have borrowed a costume from the theater!

He remembered Plato's words: *A girl will get in terrible trouble if she tries to attend the Olympic Games.*

Jack shook his head at her and pointed his finger, as if to say, *Get out of here!*

But Annie just waved at him again.

Jack kept shaking his head at Annie. He even shook his fist.

Annie turned back to watch the race.

"It's not a joke!" Jack shouted.

Plato turned and looked at him.

"Of course not," said Plato. "We take the games very seriously."

Jack felt his face grow hot. He glared at Annie's back.

Just then the trumpet sounded.

"The chariots are taking their places," said Plato.

Jack saw the dozens of chariots lined up on the race track. Each chariot was pulled by four horses.

Jack glanced back at Annie. She was looking up at him, pointing at the chariots.

The trumpet sounded again.

The horses took off!

The crowd went wild. They were cheering

and screaming and stamping their feet.

Clouds of dust rose up as the chariots raced around the track.

Annie turned back to watch the race. She began jumping up and down.

"Go! Go! Go!" she shouted.

A few people began staring at the strange small soldier with the high-pitched voice.

Jack couldn't take it anymore. He had to get Annie away before it was too late!

He shoved his notebook into his pack.

"I have to go!" he shouted to Plato.

The philosopher looked surprised.

Jack was afraid to tell him that Annie had broken the rules.

"I had a great time. But I have to go home now," said Jack. "Thanks for everything!"

"Have a safe journey," said Plato.

Jack waved and started down the steps.

As he climbed down, he saw Annie pull off her helmet.

Her pigtails flew up and down as she jumped and shouted, "Go! Go! Go!"

Her soldier's cape fell off.

Now *lots* of people were staring at her. Someone shouted for the guards.

Annie was too busy cheering to notice anything.

Jack moved as quickly as he could.

But two big guards got to Annie first.

8

Save Annie!

The guards tried to pull Annie away from the chariot race.

Annie looked surprised. Then she looked angry.

"Let go of me!" she shouted.

Jack rushed down the steps of the viewing stand.

The guards were having a hard time pulling Annie through all the people.

"Leave her alone!" Jack yelled.

His voice was lost in the noise of the race.

He pushed his way through the crowd.

"Leave her alone!" he kept shouting. "Leave her alone!"

Finally, Jack reached Annie and the guards. He tried to grab her, but a guard blocked his way.

"Let her go!" yelled Jack. "I promise I'll take her home!"

More guards arrived. The crowd began to shout, "Arrest her! Arrest her!"

The guards kept pulling Annie away.

"Jack! The story!" cried Annie.

Of course! thought Jack. *The poet's story! This is definitely our darkest hour!*

He reached into his bag and pulled out the poet's scroll.

He held the story up to the sky.

"Save Annie!" he shouted.

But Jack's voice was again lost in the roar of the race as the four-horse chariots barreled through the dust.

Jack looked around wildly for someone—or something—to help them.

Then suddenly the crowd fell silent.

All heads turned to watch as a huge white horse galloped out of the dust.

The crowd murmured with excitement and wonder.

The white horse was the most beautiful animal Jack had ever seen.

He was pulling an empty chariot.

And he was galloping straight toward Jack.

9

Fly Away Home

The white horse stopped at the low wall by the edge of the track.

"He's come for *us!*" cried Annie.

The guards stared in awe at the horse.

Annie broke free and dashed over to Jack. He grabbed her hand and they ran to the horse.

The guards shouted and started after them.

But they were too late. Jack and Annie had already climbed over the wall and into the waiting chariot.

"Go! Go! Go!" Annie cried to the huge white horse.

The horse reared and pawed the air.

The crowd stepped back from the wall.

The guards froze.

Jack looked up to where Plato was now standing. Plato smiled and waved at him.

Then the white horse leaped forward, pulling the chariot behind him.

Jack couldn't even wave back at Plato. All he could do was hold on tight as the horse galloped beside the Olympic racers.

Jack bounced up and down. Dust and sand got in his eyes. He squeezed them shut and crouched down in the chariot.

He didn't know where they were going. But it didn't matter. The white horse was in charge.

Jack heard the thundering noise of the racing horses and chariots. He heard the screaming crowd.

He felt sand blowing in his face and the hard bumping and rattling of the chariot.

Suddenly, he was thrown backward. He heard a *swoosh* of wind, then...

Silence.

"Oh, wow!" cried Annie.

Jack opened his eyes. All he saw was blue sky. He pushed his glasses into place and looked around.

"Help!" he cried.

The white horse had grown giant feathery wings and was pulling their chariot into the sky.

Jack gripped the railing of the chariot and held on for his life.

"To the tree house!" shouted Annie.

Below, the Olympic crowd watched in stunned silence.

The winged horse left the games behind and flew over the temple of Zeus, over the

statue of Nike, over the sacred olive tree and the gymnasium.

On they went: over the poet's house, the Greek theater, and the field of white tents.

Finally, the winged horse coasted to the ground near the olive grove.

The wheels of the chariot bumped onto the grass. Then slowly, slowly, they came to a stop.

Jack and Annie stepped out of the chariot. Jack's legs were so wobbly he could hardly walk.

Annie rushed to the horse and stroked his neck.

"Thank you," she whispered.

Jack patted the horse's long white neck too.

"Thanks," he said. "That was the best ride of my life."

The horse snorted and pawed the ground.

"Come on, Annie. We have to go before they find us," said Jack.

"I don't want to leave him," said Annie. "He's the most beautiful horse in the whole world."

Her eyes filled with tears.

"We have to," said Jack.

The horse put his head down and touched Annie's forehead with his soft nose. Then he gave her a gentle push toward the tree house.

Annie sniffled but started walking. Jack took her hand as they walked through the olive grove to the rope ladder of the tree house.

"You first," Jack said.

Annie started up the ladder. Jack followed.

When they were inside, Annie hurried to the window. Jack grabbed the Pennsylvania book.

He pointed to a picture of the Frog Creek woods and said, "I wish—"

"Look!" said Annie.

Jack looked out the window. The horse

had spread his great feathery wings. He was rising from the field.

The white horse flew high into the blue Olympian sky.

Then he disappeared behind the clouds.

"Bye!" called Annie.

A tear rolled down her cheek.

Jack pointed again at the Pennsylvania book.

"I wish we could go there," he said.

The wind started to blow.

The tree house began to spin.

It spun faster and faster.

Then everything was still.

Absolutely still.

10

They're All Here

Jack opened his eyes.

It was so dark he couldn't see anything.

He felt his clothes. He was wearing his T-shirt and jeans again. The leather bag had turned back into his backpack.

"Hello," said Morgan le Fay. Her voice came from the corner of the tree house.

"Hi!" said Annie.

"Did you have a good journey?" asked Morgan.

"*I* did," said Jack, "but girls can't do anything fun in ancient Greece."

"I did *one* fun thing," Annie said wistfully. "I rode in a chariot pulled by a flying horse."

"That must have been wonderful," said Morgan. "You were very lucky to be bringing me the story of Pegasus."

"Who?" said Jack.

"Pegasus," said Morgan. "He's the great white winged horse in Greek mythology."

"Oh, yeah," said Jack. "I think I've heard of him."

He felt in his backpack and found the scroll. He gave it to Morgan. He could still barely see her in the dark.

"It was written by Anonymous," said Annie.

"I know," said Morgan. "Many talented

women used that name in the past. Her story will be a great addition to my Camelot library."

"Plato helped us find it," said Jack.

"Ah, my good friend Plato," said Morgan. "He was one of the greatest thinkers who ever lived."

"And Pegasus was the greatest horse," said Annie. She sighed. "I just wish I could see him again."

"You can," Morgan said softly. "He's here right now."

"Pegasus?" cried Annie. "Oh, boy!"

Annie turned on the flashlight and used it to find her way down the rope ladder.

Jack grabbed his backpack and followed her.

When they were both standing on the

ground, Annie shined her flashlight at the dark trees.

"Pegasus?" she said. "Where are you? Pegasus?"

"Turn off your flashlight, Annie," said Morgan. She was looking down from the tree house window.

Annie switched off the light.

"In the night, you can see *all* the story characters that saved you on your last four missions," said Morgan. "They are all here— Hercules and the silk weaver, Sarph, the serpent monster and Pegasus."

Jack pushed his glasses into place and studied the dark woods.

"Where are they, Morgan?" cried Annie. "Where's Pegasus?"

"Look hard," said Morgan.

"I can't see him!" said Annie.

"Yes, you can," said Morgan. "The old stories are always with us. We are never alone."

Has Morgan gone crazy? wondered Jack.

"Look up," said Morgan. "Your friends are in the night sky. They are stars."

"Stars?" whispered Jack.

He stared at the shimmering field of tiny stars overhead.

"Hercules is a constellation," said Morgan. "The Romans imagined him kneeling in the sky, holding a club over his head."

Morgan waved her finger at the sky. For a moment Jack saw a living, breathing Hercules outlined by stars.

"And there's the silk weaver, with her beloved cowherd," said Morgan. "The ancient Chinese believed that they were two stars on either side of the Milky Way."

Morgan waved her hand again. The lovely silk weaver was outlined in the heavens.

"And long ago, the Irish believed the Milky Way itself was the serpent monster Sarph," said Morgan.

Morgan waved her hand. A giant serpent glittered through the sky.

"And the ancient Greeks named one of their constellations Pegasus," said Morgan.

She waved her hand again and the white horse's head, wings, and galloping legs glowed in the sky.

"I see him!" said Annie. Then she whispered, "I love you, Pegasus."

Jack thought he saw the stars move as if Pegasus was rearing back in the sky.

After a breathless moment of silence, Morgan lowered her arm. The night sky became a field of tiny glittering stars again.

"You have done amazing work as Master Librarians," said Morgan. "I would trust you with any important mission."

"Does that mean we're going on more trips?" asked Jack.

"Indeed it does," said Morgan. "*Many* more."

Jack smiled with relief.

"When is our next mission?" asked Annie.

"As soon as I need your help, I will send for you," said Morgan. "Go home now and rest."

"Good-bye," said Annie.

"Good-bye," said Jack.

"Farewell," said Morgan.

There was a sudden rushing of wind, then a blur of blinding light. And Morgan le Fay and the magic tree house vanished.

The night was still.

"Home?" asked Annie.

"Sure," said Jack.

As they walked between the trees, the Frog Creek woods were pitch-black.

Jack couldn't see a thing.

But he didn't ask Annie to turn on the flashlight. For once, he wasn't worried about finding his way home.

He felt as if someone—or something—was leading them through the woods.

Morgan's words came back to him: *The old*

stories are always with us. We are never alone.

Jack looked up at the stars again. They were beginning to fade in the growing light of dawn.

But he thought he could hear the beating of giant wings, somewhere high above.

MORE FACTS FOR YOU AND JACK

The Olympics

❧ The Olympics of ancient Greece were held for over a thousand years, from 776 B.C. to A.D. 394.

❧ Every four years, the games were held in several cities, including the town of Olympia, for five days in August. (The modern Olympics were named after Olympia.)

❧ For two months, all fighting and wars ceased so people could travel safely to and from the Olympics.

❧ The first modern Olympics were held in Athens, Greece, in 1896.

❧ Greek athletes believed that having a physically fit body was a way to honor their chief god, Zeus. Olympia's statue of Zeus was one of the seven wonders of the ancient world. Unfortunately, it no longer exists.

Greek Language

✺ The word *anonymous* comes from a Greek word that means "nameless."

✺ The English language has many words that were originally Greek, especially words having to do with sports, such as *gymnasium*, *marathon*, and *athlete*; words having to do with science, such as *psychology* and *astronomy*; and words related to the arts, such as *drama*, *theater*, and *scenery*.

✺ The word *museum* is also of Greek origin. Over 2,000 years ago, the Greeks built a temple to the nine goddesses known as the Muses. They called the temple the Museum.

✺ Some Greek letters are similar to ours. The Greek A is called *alpha*. The B is called *beta*. That's where we get our word *alphabet*.

Democracy

About 2,500 years ago, the Greeks adopted a system of government called a *democracy*. Under the Greek democracy, all citizens had a say in the government. At that time, however, women and slaves were not considered citizens.

Plato

Plato the philosopher lived in ancient Greece in the fourth century B.C. Plato founded a school called the Academy. In both his teachings and his writings, Plato explored the best way for a government to be set up. His ideas are still talked about today.

Zeus

Zeus was god of the skies and ruler of all the Greek gods and goddesses. Zeus and his family were called Olympians because they lived on top of a mountain called Mount Olympus. The major Greek gods and goddesses were later adopted by the Romans. Zeus was called Jupiter by the Romans.

Pegasus

In Greek mythology, a great winged horse sprang from the neck of a snake-haired monster known as Medusa. The horse was named Pegasus, which may come from a Greek word that means "spring." Pegasus was tamed by a young man named Bellerophon.

Star Myths

In ancient times, mythic characters from different world cultures were sometimes identified as patterns of stars in the night sky. Once a hero or heroine took a place in the heavens, he or she became famous forever.

Don't miss the next Magic Tree House book,
when Jack and Annie are whisked back
to the deck of the *Titanic* in

MAGIC TREE HOUSE #17

Tonight
on the
Titanic

(March 1999)

Where have *you* traveled in the

MAGIC TREE HOUSE?

The Mystery of the Tree House
(Books #1–4)

❑ **Magic Tree House #1, DINOSAURS BEFORE DARK,** in which Jack and Annie discover the tree house and travel back to the time of dinosaurs.

❑ **Magic Tree House #2, THE KNIGHT AT DAWN,** in which Jack and Annie go to the time of knights and explore a medieval castle with a hidden passage.

❑ **Magic Tree House #3, MUMMIES IN THE MORNING,** in which Jack and Annie go to ancient Egypt and get lost in a pyramid when they help a ghost queen.

❑ **Magic Tree House #4, PIRATES PAST NOON,** in which Jack and Annie travel back in time and meet some unfriendly pirates searching for buried treasure.

The Mystery of the Magic Spell
(Books #5–8)

❑ **Magic Tree House #5, NIGHT OF THE NINJAS,** in which Jack and Annie go to old Japan and learn the secrets of the ninjas.

❑ **Magic Tree House #6, AFTERNOON ON THE AMAZON,** in which Jack and Annie explore the wild rain forest of the Amazon and are greeted by giant ants, hungry crocodiles, and flesh-eating piranhas.

❑ **Magic Tree House #7, SUNSET OF THE SABERTOOTH,** in which Jack and Annie go back to the Ice Age—the world of woolly mammoths, sabertooth tigers, and a mysterious sorcerer.

❑ **Magic Tree House #8, MIDNIGHT ON THE MOON,** in which Jack and Annie go forward in time and explore the moon in a moon buggy.

The Mystery of the Ancient Riddles
(Books #9–12)

❑ **Magic Tree House #9, Dolphins at Daybreak,** in which Jack and Annie arrive on a coral reef, where they find a mini-submarine that takes them underwater into the world of sharks and dolphins.

❑ **Magic Tree House #10, Ghost Town at Sundown,** in which Jack and Annie travel to the Wild West, where they battle horse thieves, meet a kindly cowboy, and get some help from a mysterious ghost.

❑ **Magic Tree House #11, Lions at Lunchtime,** in which Jack and Annie go to the plains of Africa, where they help wild animals cross a rushing river and have a picnic with a Masai warrior.

❑ **Magic Tree House #12, Polar Bears Past Bedtime,** in which Jack and Annie go to the Arctic, where they get help from a seal hunter, play with polar bear cubs, and get trapped on thin ice.

The Mystery of the Lost Libraries
(Books #13–16)

❑ **Magic Tree House #13, VACATION UNDER THE VOLCANO,** in which Jack and Annie land in Pompeii during Roman times, on the very day that Mount Vesuvius erupts.

❑ **Magic Tree House #14, DAY OF THE DRAGON KING,** in which Jack and Annie travel back to ancient China, where they must face an emperor who burns books.

❑ **Magic Tree House #15, VIKING SHIPS AT SUNRISE,** in which Jack and Annie travel back to a monastery in medieval Ireland, where they meet a friendly monk and an unfriendly bunch of Vikings!

Read all the Magic Tree House books!

Available wherever books are sold...OR
You can send in this coupon (with check or money order)
and have the books mailed directly to you!

❏	#1: DINOSAURS BEFORE DARK (0-679-82411-1)	$3.99
❏	#2: THE KNIGHT AT DAWN (0-679-82412-X)	$3.99
❏	#3: MUMMIES IN THE MORNING (0-679-82424-3)	$3.99
❏	#4: PIRATES PAST NOON (0-679-82425-1)	$3.99
❏	#5: NIGHT OF THE NINJAS (0-679-86371-0)	$3.99
❏	#6: AFTERNOON ON THE AMAZON (0-679-86372-9)	$3.99
❏	#7: SUNSET OF THE SABERTOOTH (0-679-86373-7)	$3.99
❏	#8: MIDNIGHT ON THE MOON (0-679-86374-5)	$3.99
❏	#9: DOLPHINS AT DAYBREAK (0-679-88338-X)	$3.99
❏	#10: GHOST TOWN AT SUNDOWN (0-679-88339-8)	$3.99
❏	#11: LIONS AT LUNCHTIME (0-679-88340-1)	$3.99
❏	#12, POLAR BEARS PAST BEDTIME (0-679-88341-X)	$3.99
❏	#13: VACATION UNDER THE VOLCANO (0-679-89050-5)	$3.99
❏	#14: DAY OF THE DRAGON KING (0-679-89051-3)	$3.99
❏	#15: VIKING SHIPS AT SUNRISE (0-679-89061-0)	$3.99

Subtotal ....$ _____
Shipping and handling.............................$ 3.00
Sales tax (where applicable).................... _____
Total amount enclosed.............................$ _____

Name _____

Address _____

City _____ State _____ Zip _____

Do you love the Magic Tree House books?

**Do you want sneak previews
of the next book in the series?**

Climb the ladder into
The Magic Tree House Club!

You'll get:
- three newsletters filled with fun facts,
  games, puzzles, and a note from author
  Mary Pope Osborne
- a super Magic Tree House surprise
- plus chances to win free books and prizes

SIGN ME UP! I want to be a member of
The Magic Tree House Club.

MY NAME: _____

MY ADDRESS: _____

_____

Have an adult write a $1.50 check or money order
payable to Random House, Inc., for shipping and
handling. Send this coupon and your check or money
order to:

The Magic Tree House Club
Random House, Inc.
201 East 50th Street
Mail Drop 30-2
New York, NY 10022

Visit the

MAGIC TREE HOUSE

website

at

www.randomhouse.com/magictreehouse

Look for these other Random House books
by Mary Pope Osborne!

Picture books:
Molly and the Prince
Moonhorse

For middle-grade readers:
American Tall Tales
One World, Many Religions

And available in July 1999,
the Spider Kane mysteries!
*Spider Kane and the Mystery Under
the May-Apple (#1)*
*Spider Kane and the Mystery at
Jumbo Nightcrawler's (#2)*